Story I

The Boy Who Cried Wolf

양치기 소년

Story II

Chicken Licken

치킨 리킨

직독직해로 읽는 스토리북 ❶

Story I

The Boy Who Cried Wolf 양치기 소년

Story II

Chicken Licken 치킨 리킨

초판 1쇄 **인쇄**　2013년 10월 21일
초판 1쇄 **발행**　2013년 10월 31일

편역	이현구
편집	더 콜링_김정희
삽화	김태연, 김명희
디자인	IndigoBlue_김은경
E-Book	BASRAC
녹음	Charm (주)참미디어
성우	Grace Johnson
발행인	조경아
발행처	랭귀지북스
주소	서울시 마포구 포은로 2나길 31 벨라비스타 208호
전화	070.4123.3640 / 02.406.0047
팩스	02.406.0042
이메일	languagebooks@hanmail.net
홈페이지	www.languagebooks.co.kr
등록번호	101-90-85278
등록일자	2008년 7월 10일
ISBN	978-89-94145-93-8 (18740)
가격	9,800원

ⓒ Language Books 2013

Story I

The Boy Who Cried Wolf

양치기 소년

Story II

Chicken Licken

치킨 리킨

Language Books

About This Storybook

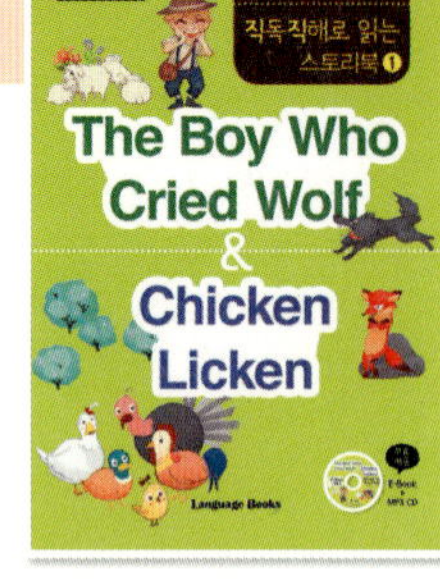

Story

녹음을 들으며 본문을 잘 읽어 보세요.
원어민의 발음과 억양에 주의하여 따라 해 보세요.

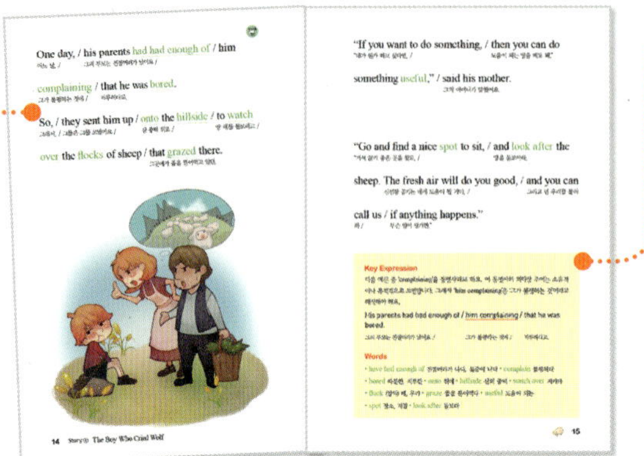

Key Expression & Words

본문 중에 꼭 익혀야 할
주요 표현을 뽑았어요.
그리고 사전 없이 쉽게
읽을 수 있도록 다양한
어휘를 수록했어요.

Mini Test

간단한 문제들을 통해
읽은 내용에 대해
얼마나 이해했는지
확인해 보세요.

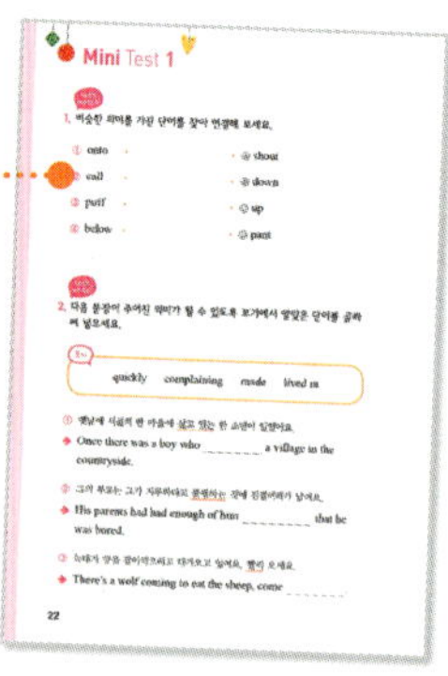

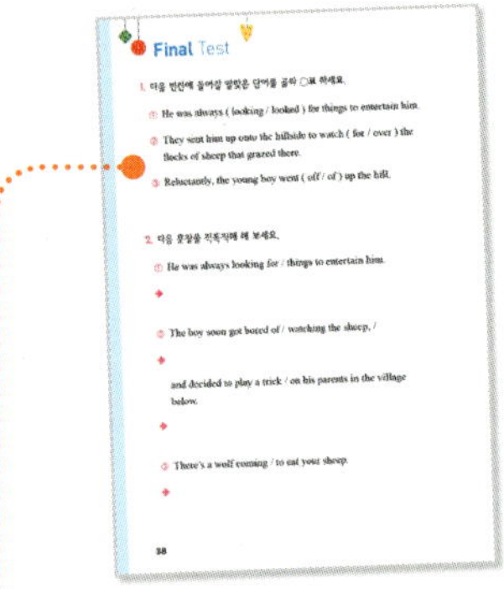

Read the Story in the original

직독직해로 읽은 내용을 바탕으로
원문으로 다시 읽어 보세요.
해석과 단어 없이 녹음을 들으며
얼마나 이해할 수 있는지 알아보세요.

Final Test

여러 가지 활동을 통해
전체 이야기에 대한
이해력을 높이고
내 실력을 점검해 보세요.

About This E-Book

Intro

❶ 학습하고자 하는
코너를 클릭하세요.

❷ 녹음 파일만
따로 모아 두었어요.

E-Book Story

❸ 해당 코너로
바로 이동할 수 있어요.

❹ 녹음 속도를 1~3단계로
조절할 수 있어요.

❺ 다음 페이지로 넘어가요.

❻ 모르는 단어는
바로 확인할 수 있어요.

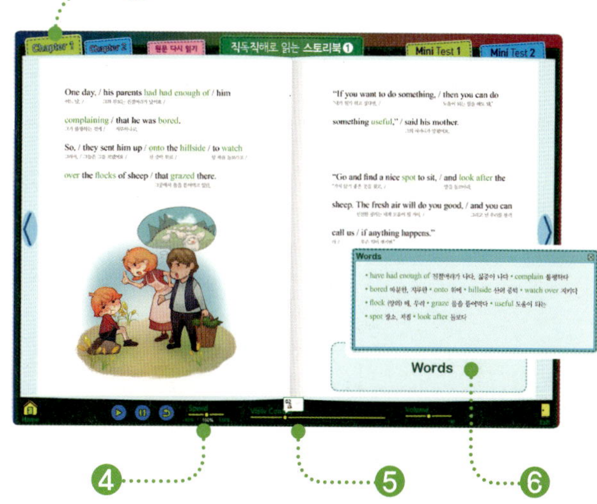

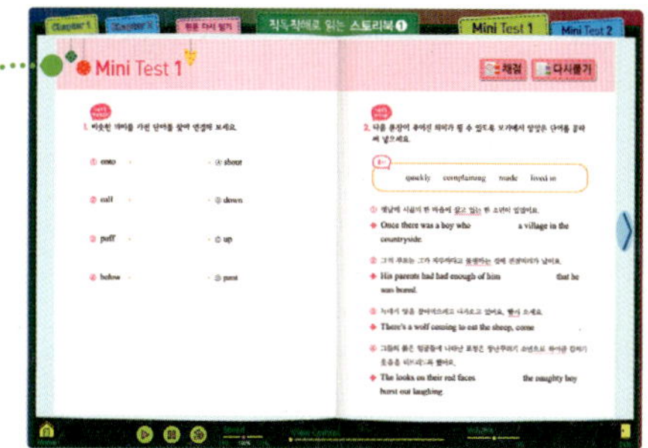

Mini Test

어휘, 듣기, 독해 등 다양한 문제를
직접 풀어 보며 실력을 확인할 수 있어요.

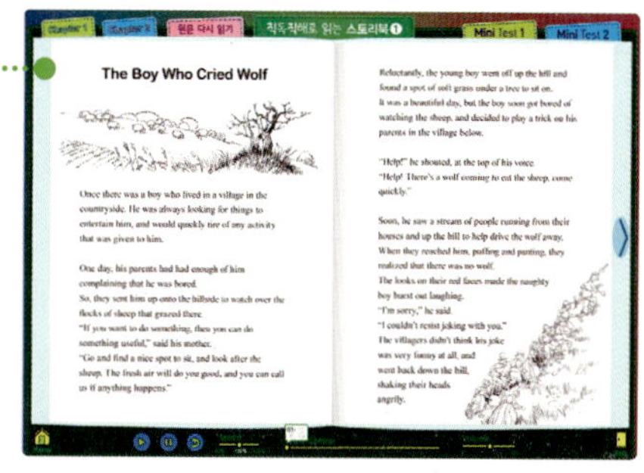

원문 다시 읽기

원어민이 읽어 주는 이야기를
처음부터 끝까지 다시 들을 수 있어요.

About Storybook Handwritng

따라쓰기 별매

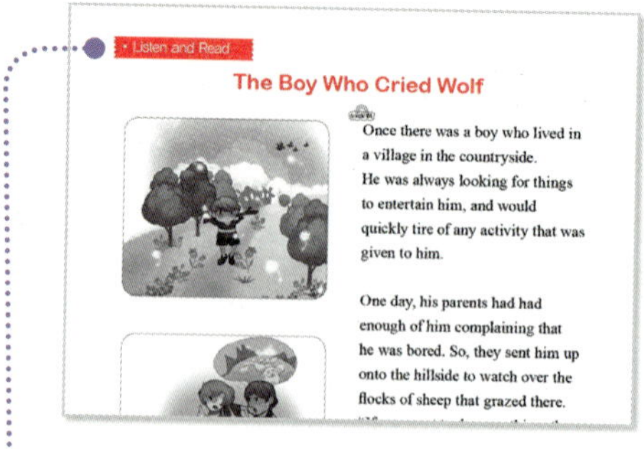

• Listen and Read

원어민의 녹음을 들으며
본문을 잘 읽어 보세요.

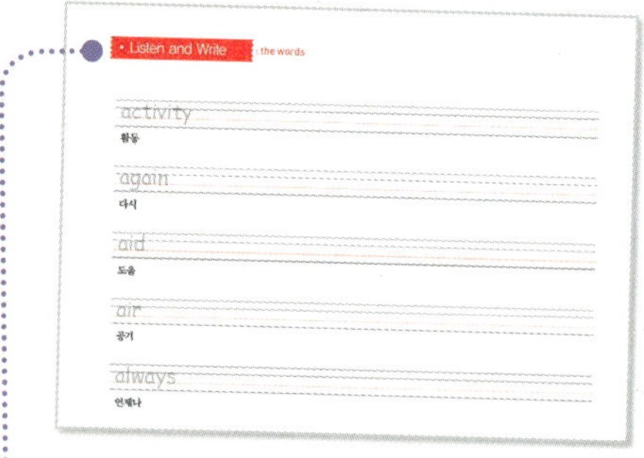

• Listen and Write : the words

이야기에 나오는 기본 단어를
따라 쓰며 익히세요.

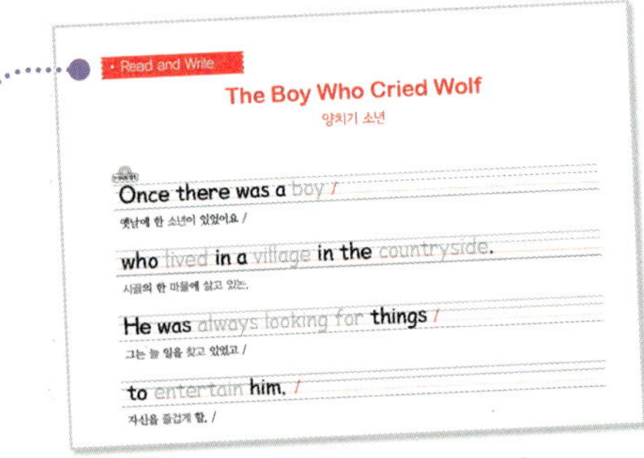

• Read and Write

영어 어순대로 문장을 끊어
직독직해 하면서 따라 써 보세요.

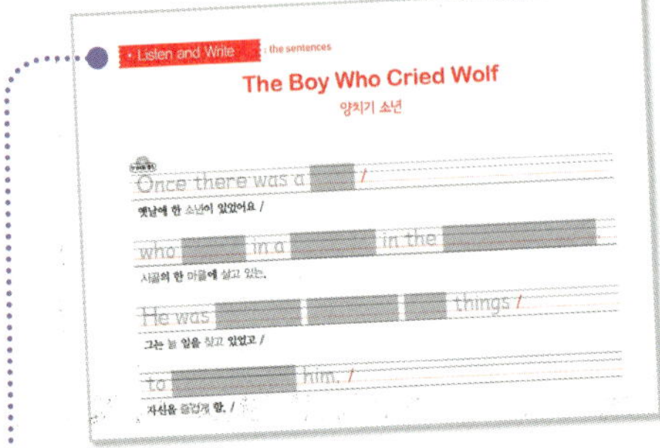

• Listen and Write : the sentences

녹음을 들으며 빈칸에
알맞은 단어/구문을 써 넣으세요.

• Listen and Write : the story

앞에서 익힌 내용을 바탕으로
영어로 이야기를 만들어 보세요.

Contents

Story Ⅰ The Boy Who Cried Wolf 양치기 소년

Chapter 1 — 12
Mini Test 1 — 22

Chapter 2 — 24
Mini Test 2 — 32

원문 읽기
The Boy Who Cried Wolf — 34

Final Test — 38

Story Ⅱ Chicken Licken 치킨 리킨

Chapter 1 — 44
Mini Test 1 — 58

Chapter 2 — 60
Mini Test 2 — 74

원문 읽기
Chicken Licken — 76

Final Test — 82

Index — 86

Story I The Boy Who Cried Wolf
양치기 소년

* The Boy

장난치기만 좋아하는 소년은
무엇을 하든 금방 싫증을 낸다.
날씨 좋은 날, 산 위에서
양 떼를 돌보는 일에 지루함을 느껴
마을 사람들에게 거짓말을 하는데…….

* The Villagers

무슨 일이든 자신의 일처럼
적극 도와주는 착한 사람들.
소년의 거짓 외침에 속아
산 위에 여러 번 올라가는데…….

Story Ⅱ Chicken Licken
치킨 리킨

* Chicken Liken

덜렁대는 성격 때문에 자주 실수를 저지른다.
어느 날, 머리에 떨어진 도토리가
하늘의 조각인 줄 알고 깜짝 놀라는데…….

* Cocky Locky

남의 말을 쉽게 믿는 편이라
치킨 리킨의 말만 듣고
바로 동행을 결심한다.

* Ducky Lucky

늘 미리 걱정을 하는 탓에
섣부른 판단을 내리고
치킨 리킨의 여행에 함께한다.

* Goosey Lucy

남을 잘 따라 하는 편이라
친구들의 행렬에
주저없이 동참한다.

* Turkey Lurkey

늘 과장스러운 칠면조는
치킨 리킨의 행렬에
호들갑을 떨며 끼어든다.

* Foxy Loxy

음흉하고 교활한 여우는
순진한 치킨 리킨 일행을
도와주는 척 안심시키며 접근한다.

양치기 소년

양치기 소년

The Boy Who Cried Wolf

Chapter 1

Once there was a boy / who lived in a village in the
옛날에 한 소년이 있었어요 /   시골의 한 마을에 살고 있는.

countryside. He was always looking for things /
그는 늘 일을 찾고 있었고 /

to entertain him, / and would quickly tire of / any
자신을 즐겁게 할, /   빨리 싫증을 내곤 했어요 /

activity that was given to him.
그에게 주어진 어떤 활동이든.

Words

• village (시골) 마을 • countryside 시골, 지방 • look for 찾다

• entertain 즐겁게 하다 • quickly 빨리 • tire of 싫증을 내다 • activity 활동

track 02

One day, / his parents had had enough of / him
어느 날, / 그의 부모는 진절머리가 났어요 /

complaining / that he was bored.
그가 불평하는 것에 / 지루하다고.

So, / they sent him up / onto the hillside / to watch
그래서, / 그들은 그를 보냈어요 / 산 중턱 위로 / 양 떼를 돌보라고 /

over the flocks of sheep / that grazed there.
그곳에서 풀을 뜯어먹고 있던.

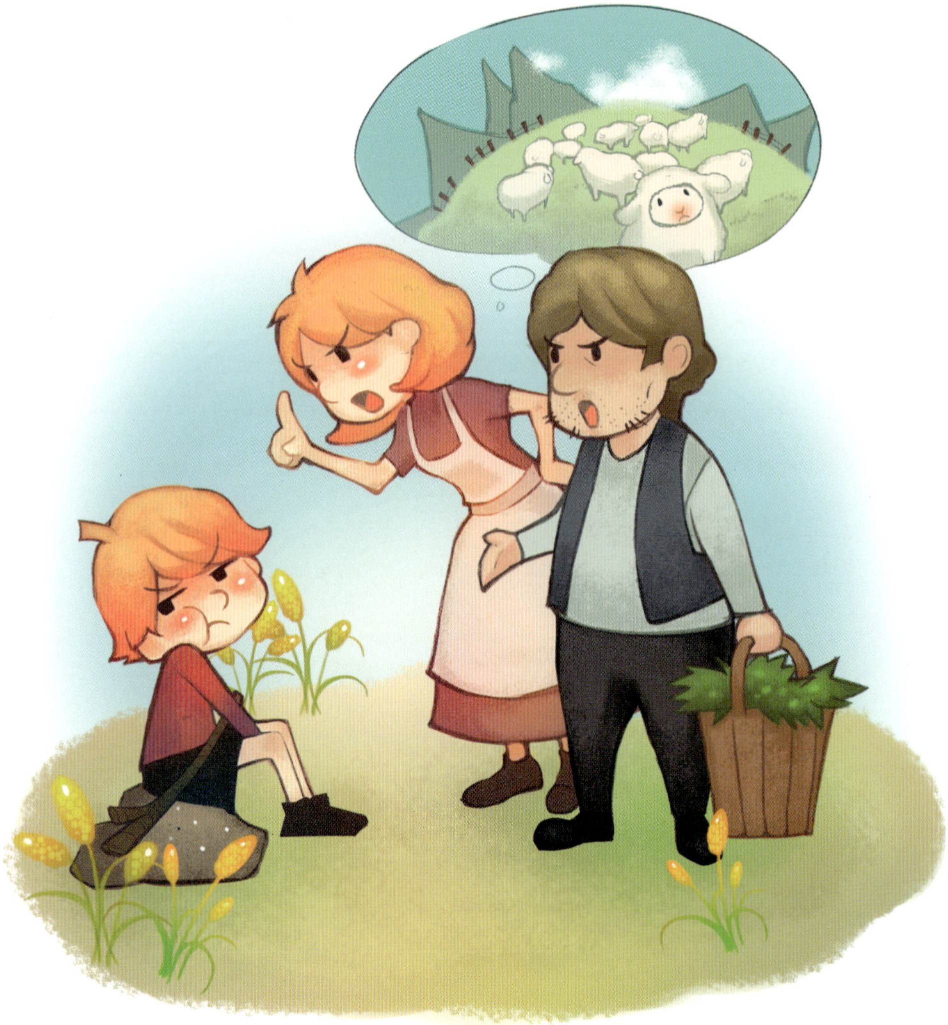

"If you want to do something, / then you can do
"네가 뭔가 하고 싶다면, /   도움이 되는 일을 해도 돼,"

something useful," / said his mother.
                그의 어머니가 말했어요.

"Go and find a nice spot to sit, / and look after the
"가서 앉기 좋은 곳을 찾고, /   양을 돌보아라.

sheep. The fresh air will do you good, / and you can
        신선한 공기는 네게 도움이 될 거야, /   그리고 넌 우리를 불러

call us / if anything happens."
라 /   무슨 일이 생기면."

Key Expression

다음 예문 중 'complaining'을 동명사라고 해요. 이 동명사의 의미상 주어는 소유격
이나 목적격으로 쓰인답니다. 그래서 'him complaining'은 '그가 불평하는 것'이라고
해석해야 해요.

His parents had had enough of / him complaining / that he was
bored.

그의 부모는 진절머리가 났어요 /   그가 불평하는 것에 /   지루하다고.

Words

• have had enough of 진절머리가 나다, 싫증이 나다 • complain 불평하다

• bored 따분한, 지루한 • onto 위에 • hillside 산의 중턱 • watch over 지키다

• flock (양의) 떼, 무리 • graze 풀을 뜯어먹다 • useful 도움이 되는

• spot 장소, 지점 • look after 돌보다

 Story I   The Boy Who Cried Wolf

Reluctantly, / the young boy went off up the hill /
어쩔 수 없이, / 어린 소년은 산 위로 올라가서 /

and found a spot of soft grass / under a tree / to sit
연한 풀이 있는 곳을 찾았어요 / 나무 아래 / 앉으려고.

on. It was a beautiful day, / but the boy soon got
날씨는 좋았어요, / 하지만 소년은 금방 싫증이 났고 /

bored of / watching the sheep, / and decided to play
양을 돌보는 일에, / 그래서 장난을 하기로 결심했어요 /

a trick / on his parents in the village below.
마을 아래에 있는 부모에게.

Words

• reluctantly 마지못해, 어쩔 수 없이 • decide to ~하기로 결심하다
• play a trick on ~에게 장난을 하다 • below 아래에

 Story 1   The Boy Who Cried Wolf

"Help!" / he shouted, / at the top of his voice.
"도와주세요!" / 그는 소리쳤어요, / 목청껏.

"Help! There's a wolf coming / to eat the sheep, /
"도와주세요! 늑대가 다가오고 있어요 / 양을 잡아먹으려고, /

come quickly."
빨리 오세요."

Soon, / he saw / a stream of people running / from
곧, / 소년은 봤어요 / 한 줄로 늘어선 사람들이 /

their houses / and up the hill / to help drive the wolf
집에서 뛰어나와 / 산 위로 올라오는 것을 / 늑대를 쫓아내는 것을 도우려고.

away.

Words

• shout 외치다 • at the top of one's voice 목청껏, 최대의 목소리로

• a stream of 한 줄로 늘어선 • drive ~ away ~을 쫓아내다, 몰아내다

track 05

When they reached him, / puffing and panting, /
사람들이 그에게 이르렀을 때, / 숨이 차서 헐떡거리며, /

they realized / that there was no wolf.
깨달았어요 / 늑대가 없다는 것을.

The looks on their red faces / made the naughty boy
그들의 붉은 얼굴들에 나타난 표정은 / 장난꾸러기 소년으로 하여금 웃음을 터뜨

burst out laughing.
리도록 했어요.

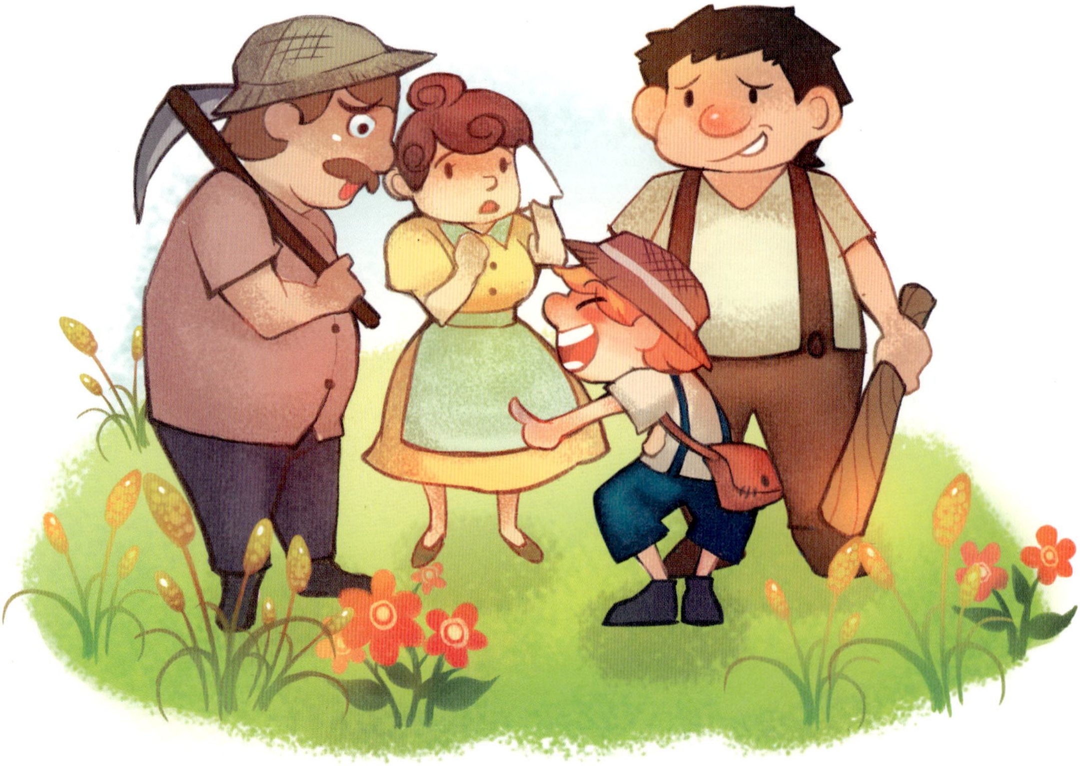

"I'm sorry," / he said.
"죄송해요." /   그가 말했어요.

"I couldn't resist / joking with you."
"전 참을 수 없었어요 /   장난을 치고 싶어서."

The villagers didn't think / his joke was very funny
마을 사람들은 생각하지 않았고 /   그의 장난이 조금도 재미있다고, /

at all, / and went back down the hill, / shaking their
산 아래로 돌아갔어요, /   화가 나서 고개를 저으며.

heads angrily.

Key Expression

다음 예문에서 동사 'make'는 '~가 …하게 하다, ~로 하여금 …하게 하다'라는 의미로 사용되었어요. 이런 경우, 'make+목적어+동사원형'의 형태로 쓰인답니다.

The looks on their red faces / made the naughty boy burst out laughing.

그들의 붉은 얼굴들에 나타난 표정은 / 장난꾸러기 소년으로 하여금 웃음을 터뜨리도록 했어요.

Words

• reach ~에 이르다 • puff (숨을) 헐떡이다 • pant 헐떡거리다

• realize 깨닫다, 알아차리다 • look 표정 • naughty 장난꾸러기의

• burst out laughing 웃음을 터뜨리다 • resist 참다 • villager 마을 사람

• shake head 고개를 젓다 • angrily 노하여, 성나서

Mini Test 1

1. 비슷한 의미를 가진 단어를 찾아 연결해 보세요.

① onto   •

② call   •

③ puff   •

④ below   •

• Ⓐ shout

• Ⓑ down

• Ⓒ up

• Ⓓ pant

2. 다음 문장이 주어진 의미가 될 수 있도록 보기에서 알맞은 단어를 골라 써 넣으세요.

> quickly   complaining   made   lived in

① 옛날에 시골의 한 마을에 <u>살고 있는</u> 한 소년이 있었어요.

➡ Once there was a boy who ___________ a village in the countryside.

② 그의 부모는 그가 지루하다고 <u>불평하는</u> 것에 진절머리가 났어요.

➡ His parents had had enough of him ___________ that he was bored.

③ 늑대가 양을 잡아먹으려고 다가오고 있어요, <u>빨리</u> 오세요.

➡ There's a wolf coming to eat the sheep, come ___________ .

④ 그들의 붉은 얼굴들에 나타난 표정은 장난꾸러기 소년<u>으로 하여금</u> 갑자기 웃음을 터뜨리도록 <u>했어요</u>.

➡ The looks on their red faces ＿＿＿＿＿＿ the naughty boy burst out laughing.

3. 다음 녹음을 듣고, 보기에서 빈칸에 알맞은 단어를 골라 써 넣으세요.

> decided   angrily   spot   look
> trick   shaking   drive   stream

① "Go and find a nice ＿＿＿＿＿ to sit, and ＿＿＿＿＿ after the sheep. The fresh air will do you good, and you can call us if anything happens."

② It was a beautiful day, but the boy soon got bored of watching the sheep, and ＿＿＿＿＿ to play a ＿＿＿＿＿ on his parents in the village below.

③ He saw a ＿＿＿＿＿ of people running from their houses and up the hill to help ＿＿＿＿＿ the wolf away.

④ The villagers didn't think his joke was very funny at all, and went back down the hill, ＿＿＿＿＿ their heads ＿＿＿＿＿.

Answer
1. ①-ⓒ / ②-Ⓐ / ③-Ⓓ / ④-Ⓑ
2. ① lived in ② complaining ③ quickly ④ made
3. ① spot / look ② decided / trick ③ stream / drive ④ shaking / angrily

Chapter 2

Before too long, / the boy was bored / once again.
머지않아, / 소년은 따분해졌어요 / 또 다시

"Help!" / he shouted.
"도와주세요!" / 그가 소리쳤어요.

"There's a wolf coming / to eat your sheep."
"늑대가 다가오고 있어요 / 양을 잡아먹으려고."

Sure enough, / the villagers stopped / what they
예상한 대로 / 마을 사람들은 멈추고 / 하던 일을 /

were doing / and ran up the hill / to the boy's aid.
산 위로 달려왔어요 / 소년을 도와주려고.

Words

• before too long 머지않아, 곧 • once again 또 다시, 한 번 더

• sure enough 예상한 대로, 예측한대로 • aid (특정 인물에 대한) 도움

track 07

He laughed and laughed / until his stomach hurt.
그는 웃고 또 웃었어요 / 배가 아플 정도로.

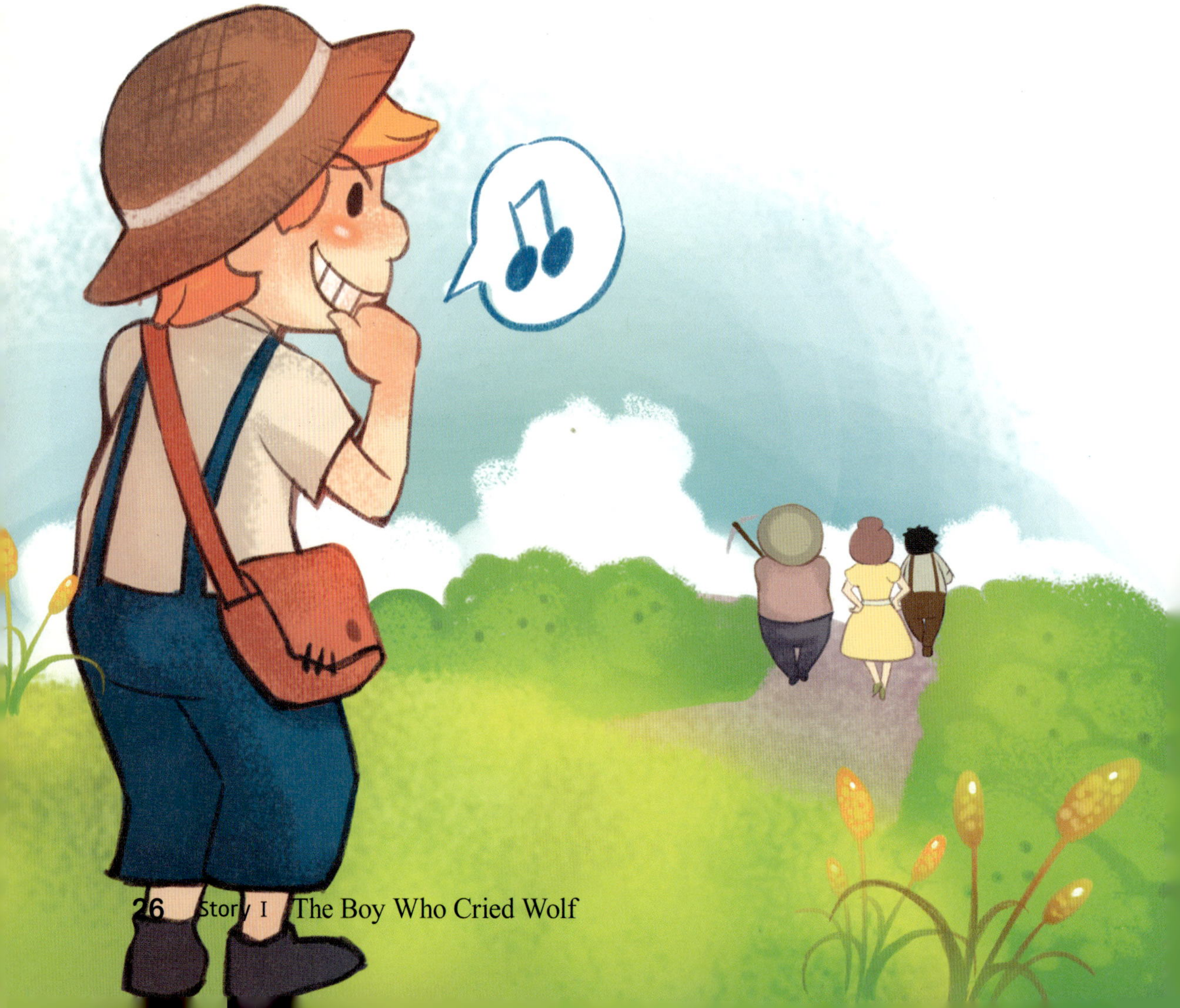

"I'm sorry," / he said, / once he had managed to get
"죄송해요," /   그가 말했어요, /   그는 겨우 한 번 숨을 돌리며.

his breath back.

"It was just too tempting / to trick you all again."
"너무 하고 싶었거든요 /   여러분에게 또 장난치는 것을."

Without a word, / the villagers turned, / and went
아무 말도 하지 않고, /   마을 사람들은 방향을 바꾸어, /

back to their houses, / leaving the boy alone again.
그들의 집으로 돌아갔어요, /   또 소년을 홀로 남겨 두고.

Suddenly, / he saw / a big, black shape slinking /
갑자기, /　　　　그는 봤어요 /　크고 검은 모습을 한 것이 살금살금 걷고 있는 것을 /

between the trees, / and his heart started to race.
나무 사이로, /　　　　그러자 그의 심장이 뛰기 시작했어요.

"Wolf!" / he called, / as loudly as he could.
"늑대야!" /　　　그는 외쳤어요, /　가능한 큰 소리로.

"Come back. There's a wolf coming / to eat the
"돌아오세요.　　늑대가 다가오고 있어요 /　　　　양을 잡아먹으려고."

sheep."

But no one came.
하지만 아무도 오지 않았어요.

Words

• slink 살금살금 가다 • race (심장이) 뛰다

track 09

All the doors to the houses stayed shut.
모든 집의 문들은 닫힌 채로 있었어요.

You see, / the villagers all thought / he was trying to trick them again.
여러분이 알듯이, / 마을 사람들 모두 생각했어요 / 그가 또 장난을 치고 있다고.

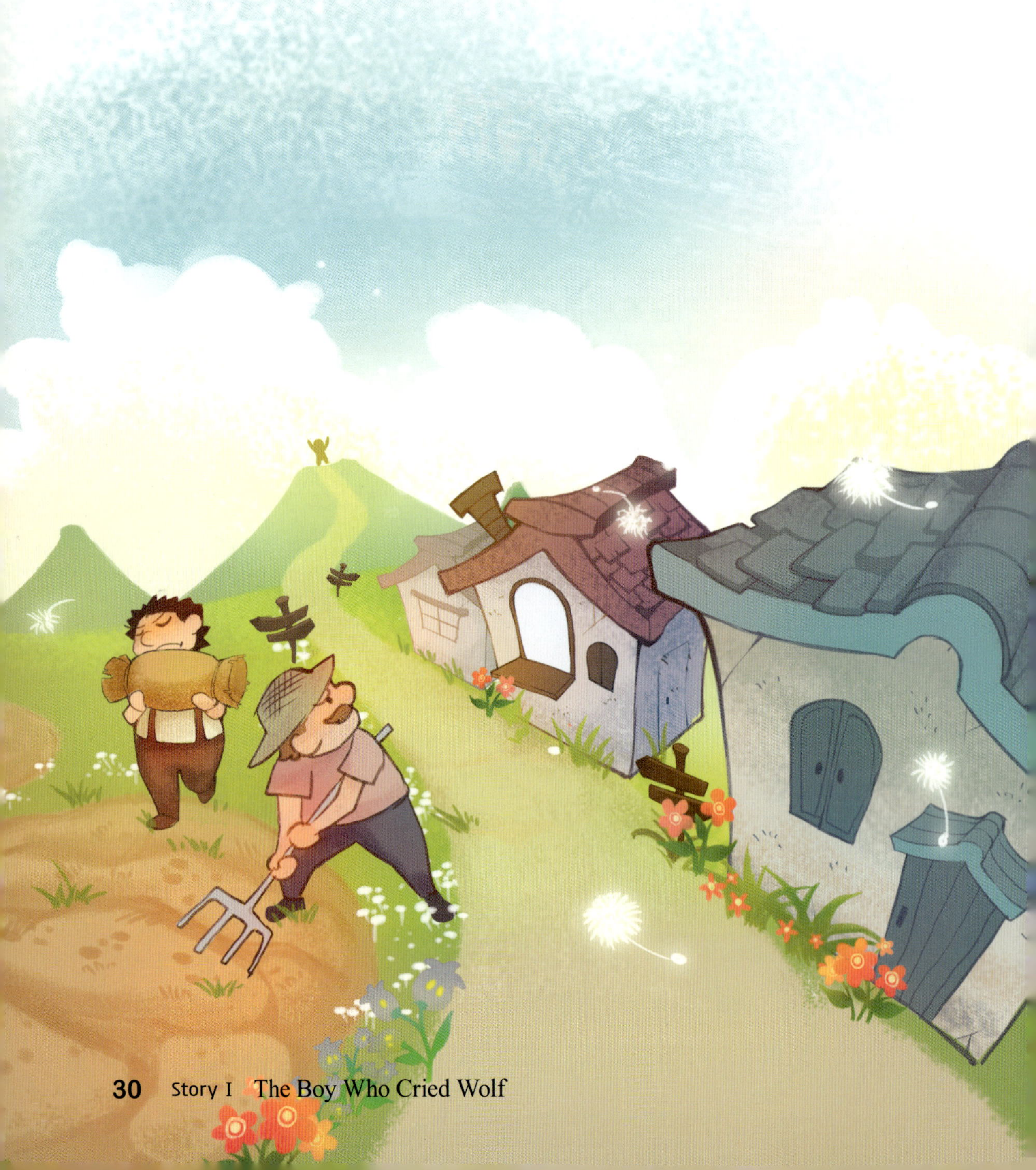

The wolf had an extra special meal / that day.
늑대는 추가로 특별한 식사를 했어요 /   그날.

First he feasted on / the sheep.
먼저 늑대는 마음껏 잡아먹었어요 /   양들을.

Then he finished his lunch / by gobbling up the
그리고 점심 식사를 마쳤어요 /   장난꾸러기 소년을 잡아먹음으로써 /

naughty boy / who cried "Wolf!"
           "늑대야!"라고 외쳤던 (소년을)

Key Expression

동사 'stay' 뒤에 형용사가 오면, '~한 채로 있다'라는 의미로, 어떤 상황이 지속되는 것을 표현합니다.

All the doors to the houses stayed shut.

모든 집의 문들은 닫힌 채로 있었어요.

Words

• shut (문이) 닫히다 • extra 추가의 • meal 식사 • feast 마음껏 먹다
• gobble up 잡아먹다

Mini Test 2

1. 다음 단어 중 밑줄친 부분의 발음이 나머지 셋과 다른 것을 고르세요.

① Ⓐ br<u>ea</u>k   Ⓑ f<u>ea</u>st   Ⓒ <u>ea</u>t   Ⓓ l<u>ea</u>ve

② Ⓐ l<u>ou</u>dly   Ⓑ en<u>ou</u>gh   Ⓒ sh<u>ou</u>t   Ⓓ h<u>ou</u>se

③ Ⓐ call<u>ed</u>   Ⓑ turn<u>ed</u>   Ⓒ start<u>ed</u>   Ⓓ stay<u>ed</u>

④ Ⓐ bl<u>a</u>ck   Ⓑ m<u>a</u>nage   Ⓒ b<u>a</u>ck   Ⓓ <u>a</u>gain

2. 다음 문장이 주어진 의미가 될 수 있도록 보기에서 알맞은 단어를 골라 써 넣으세요.

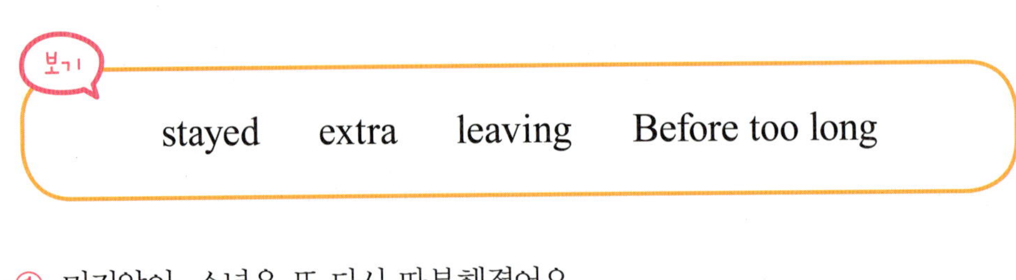

① 머지않아, 소년은 또 다시 따분해졌어요.

➡ ________________________, the boy was bored once again.

② 마을 사람들은 또 다시 소년을 홀로 남겨 두고 집으로 돌아갔어요.

➡ The villagers went back to their houses, ________ the boy alone again.

③ 모든 집의 문들은 닫힌 채로 있었어요.

➡ All the doors to the houses ________ shut.

④ 그날 늑대는 <u>추가로</u> 특별한 식사를 했어요.

➡ The wolf had an __________ special meal that day.

3. 다음 녹음을 듣고, 보기에서 빈칸에 알맞은 단어를 골라 써 넣으세요.

> 보기
>
> | slinking | gobbling | aid | managed |
> | race | enough | naughty |

① Sure __________, the villagers stopped what they were doing and ran up the hill to the boy's __________.

② "I'm sorry," he said, once he had __________ to get his breath back.

③ Suddenly, he saw a big, black shape __________ between the trees, and his heart started to __________.

④ Then he finished his lunch by __________ up the __________ boy who cried "Wolf!"

 1. ①-Ⓐ / ②-Ⓑ / ③-Ⓒ / ④-Ⓓ

2. ① Before too long ② leaving ③ stayed ④ extra

3. ① enough / aid ② managed ③ slinking / race ④ gobbling / naughty

The Boy Who Cried Wolf

Once there was a boy who lived in a village in the
countryside. He was always looking for things to
entertain him, and would quickly tire of any activity
that was given to him.

One day, his parents had had enough of him
complaining that he was bored.
So, they sent him up onto the hillside to watch over the
flocks of sheep that grazed there.
"If you want to do something, then you can do
something useful," said his mother.
"Go and find a nice spot to sit, and look after the
sheep. The fresh air will do you good, and you can call
us if anything happens."

Reluctantly, the young boy went off up the hill and found a spot of soft grass under a tree to sit on.

It was a beautiful day, but the boy soon got bored of watching the sheep, and decided to play a trick on his parents in the village below.

"Help!" he shouted, at the top of his voice.
"Help! There's a wolf coming to eat the sheep, come quickly."

Soon, he saw a stream of people running from their houses and up the hill to help drive the wolf away.
When they reached him, puffing and panting, they realized that there was no wolf.
The looks on their red faces made the naughty boy burst out laughing.
"I'm sorry," he said.
"I couldn't resist joking with you."
The villagers didn't think his joke was very funny at all, and went back down the hill, shaking their heads angrily.

Before too long, the boy was bored once again.

"Help!" he shouted.

"There's a wolf coming to eat your sheep."

Sure enough, the villagers stopped what they were
doing and ran up the hill to the boy's aid.

He laughed and laughed until his stomach hurt.

"I'm sorry," he said, once he had managed to get his
breath back.

"It was just too tempting to trick you all again."

Without a word, the villagers turned, and went back to
their houses, leaving the boy alone again.

Suddenly, he saw a big, black shape slinking between
the trees, and his heart started to race.

"Wolf!" he called, as loudly as he could.

"Come back. There's a wolf coming to eat the sheep."

But no one came.

All the doors to the houses stayed shut.

You see, the villagers all thought he was trying to trick
them again.

The wolf had an extra special meal that day. First he
feasted on the sheep.

Then he finished his lunch by gobbling up the naughty
boy who cried "Wolf!"

Final Test

1. 다음 빈칸에 들어갈 알맞은 단어를 골라 ○표 하세요.

① He was always (looking / looked) for things to entertain him.

② They sent him up onto the hillside to watch (for / over) the flocks of sheep that grazed there.

③ Reluctantly, the young boy went (off / of) up the hill.

2. 다음 문장을 직독직해 해 보세요.

① He was always looking for / things to entertain him.

➜

② The boy soon got bored of / watching the sheep, /

➜

and decided to play a trick / on his parents in the village below.

➜

③ There's a wolf coming / to eat your sheep.

➜

3. 다음 문장을 영작해 보세요.

① 네가 뭔가를 하고 싶다면, / 도움이 되는 일을 해도 돼.

➡

② 전 참을 수 없었어요 / 여러분에게 장난을 치고 싶어서.

➡

③ 아무 말도 하지 않고, / 마을 사람들은 방향을 바꾸어, /

➡

그들의 집으로 돌아갔어요.

➡

Answer
1. ① looking ② over ③ off
2. ① 그는 늘 일을 찾고 있었어요 / 자신을 즐겁게 할.
   ② 소년은 금방 싫증이 났고 / 양을 돌보는 일에, /
      그래서 장난을 하기로 결심했어요 / 마을 아래에 있는 부모에게.
   ③ 늑대가 다가오고 있어요 / 양을 잡아먹으려고.
3. ① If you want to do something, / then you can do something useful.
   ② I couldn't resist / joking with you.
   ③ Without a word, / the villagers turned, / and went back to their houses.

4. 다음 문장이 주어진 의미가 될 수 있도록 빈칸에 알맞은 말을 써 넣어 보세요.

① "도와주세요!" 그는 목청껏 소리쳤어요.

➜ "Help!" he shouted, __________________.

② 소년은 한 줄로 늘어선 사람들이 집에서 뛰어나와 산 위로 올라오는 것을 봤어요.

➜ He saw __________________ people running from their houses and up the hill.

③ "죄송해요," 그가 겨우 한 번 숨을 돌리며 말했어요.

➜ "I'm sorry," he said, once he had managed to __________ __________.

5. 다음 문장이 본문의 내용과 맞으면 T, 틀리면 F에 ✔표 하세요.

① His parents didn't want the boy to go off up the hill.

(T / F)

② The boy was tired of watching over the flocks of sheep, and he fell asleep at the hill.

(T / F)

③ The villagers realized that the boy joked with them, they went back down the hill.

(T / F)

6. 다음 빈칸에 들어갈 알맞은 말을 보기에서 골라 이야기를 완성해 보세요.

보기

| again | bored | countryside | flocks | gobbled |
| joked | sent | shouted | Suddenly | trick |

The boy was always ①___________, who lived in a village in the ②___________.

One day, his parents ③___________ him up onto the hill to watch over the ④___________ of sheep.

But the boy wanted to play a ⑤___________ on the villagers, and he ⑥___________ with them twice.

⑦___________, the wolf was coming to eat the sheep, the boy ⑧___________.

But no one came to help him, because the villagers thought the boy was trying to trick them ⑨___________.

Finally, the wolf ⑩___________ up the boy and sheep.

 4. ① at the top of his voice ② a stream of ③ get his breath back
5. ① F ② F ③ T
6. ① bored ② countryside ③ sent ④ flocks ⑤ trick ⑥ joked
⑦ Suddenly ⑧ shouted ⑨ again ⑩ gobbled

치킨
리킨

Chicken Licken

track 13

Chapter 1

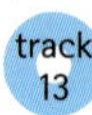

Once upon a time, / Chicken Licken was scratching
옛날 옛적에, / 치킨 리킨은 이리저리 헤집고 있었어요 /

around / in the dust of the farmyard / looking for
농가의 안마당 흙먼지를 / 맛있는 것을 찾으며 /

something tasty / to eat.
먹을 만한.

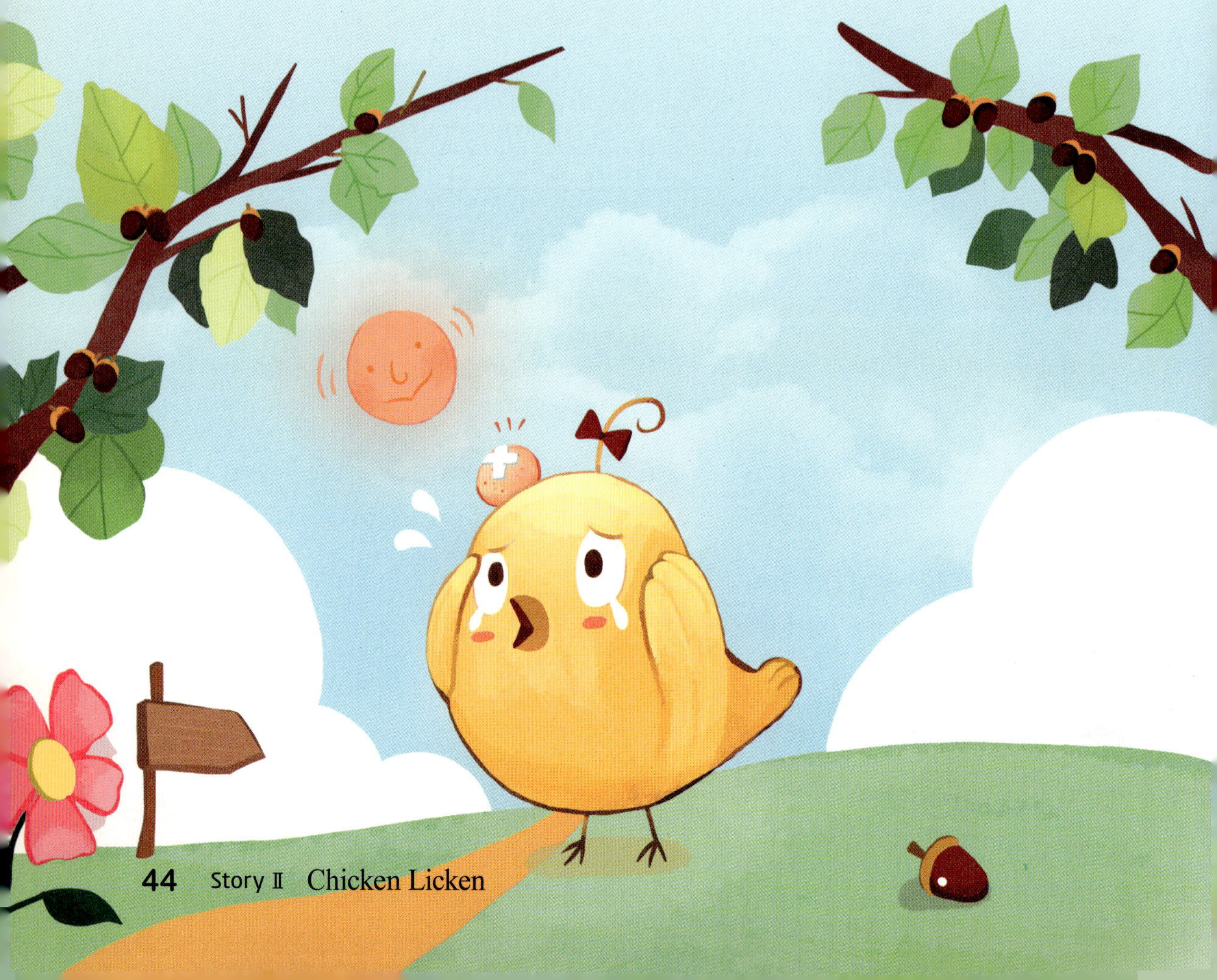

Suddenly, / an acorn fell / from a nearby tree / and
갑자기, / 도토리 한 개가 떨어지면서 / 근처의 나무에서 /

landed on her head / with a clonk.
머리 위로 내려왔어요 / 쿵하는 소리를 내며.

"Oh my!" / squawked Chicken Licken, / rubbing her
"오 이런!" / 치킨 리킨은 꽥꽥거렸어요, / 머리를 문지르며.

head.

Words

- scratch around 이리저리 헤집다 • dust 흙먼지 • farmyard 농가의 안마당
- look for 찾다 • tasty 맛있다 • acorn 도토리 • nearby 근처의
- land 떨어지다, 착륙하다 • clonk 쿵하는 소리 • squawk 꽥꽥거리다
- rub 문지르다

"The sky is falling down. I must go and tell /
"하늘이 무너지고 있어.　　　　　　　난 가서 말해야 해 /

the King / at once."
왕에게 /　　　즉시."

So off she went, / as fast as her short little legs
그래서 치킨 리킨은 출발했어요, / 짧고 작은 다리로 걸을 수 있는 한 가능한 빠르게.

would carry her.

Before very long, / she met Cocky Locky.
곧, /　　　　　　　치킨 리킨은 코키 로키를 만났어요.

"Hello there, Chicken Licken," / said Cocky Locky.
"안녕, 치킨 리킨," /　　　　　　　코키 로키가 말했어요.

"Where are you going / on this fine day?"
"어디로 가고 있니 /　　　　이렇게 날씨가 좋은 날에?"

"It is not a fine day at all, / Cocky Locky.
"전혀 날씨가 좋은 날이 아니야, /   코키 로키.

The sky is falling down. A piece of it / hit me on my
하늘이 무너지고 있어.   하늘의 한 조각이 /   내 머리를 쳤거든, /

head, / and I am going / to tell the King."
그래서 가는 중이야 /   왕에게 말하려고."

"Goodness, / Chicken Licken, / that does sound
"어머나, /   치킨 리킨, /   심각하구나." /

serious," / said Cocky Locky, / frowning.
코키 로키가 말했어요, /   얼굴을 찌푸리면서.

"May I come with you?"
"너와 함께 가도 될까?"

"Of course you may," / said Chicken Licken to
"당연하지," /   치킨 리킨이 코키 로키에게 말했어요, /

Cocky Locky, / and off they went / to see the King /
그리고 그들은 출발을 했어요 /   왕을 만나서 /

and tell him / that the sky was falling.
말하려고 /   하늘이 무너지고 있다고.

track 16

They had not got very far / when they met Ducky
그들은 별로 멀리 가지 않았어요 / 그들이 덕키 럭키를 만났을 때, /

Lucky, / who was splashing around / in the pond.
첨벙거리고 있던 / 연못에서.

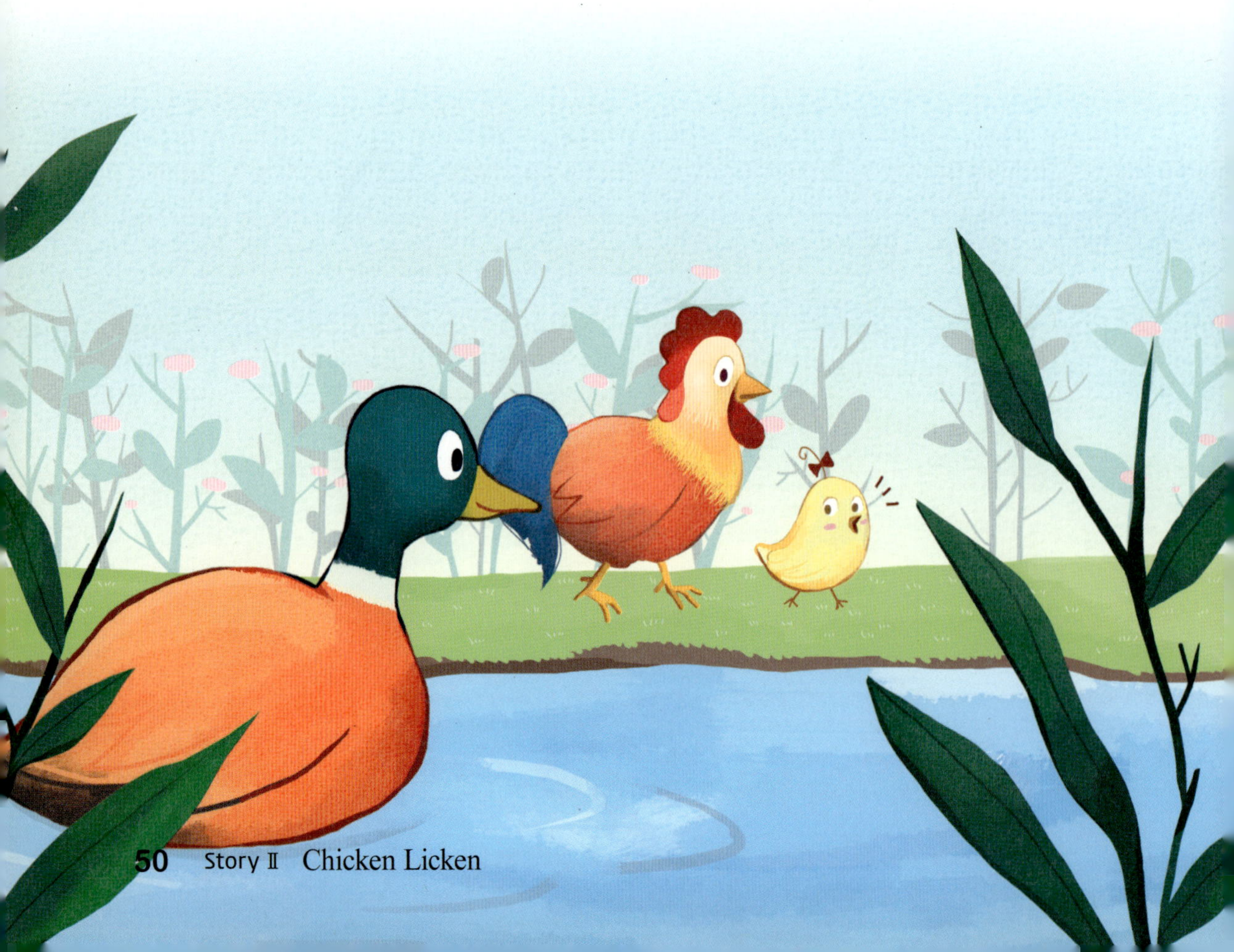

"Hello there, you two," / said Ducky Lucky to
"이봐, 거기 둘," /   덕키 럭키는 치킨 리킨과 코키 로키에게

Chicken Licken and Cocky Locky.
말했어요.

"Where are you going / in such a hurry?"
"어디로 가고 있니? /   그렇게 서둘러"

"Oh, Ducky Lucky," / said Cocky Locky, / "the sky
"오, 덕키 럭키야," /   코키 로키가 말했어요, /   "하늘이 무너지고

is falling down. A piece of it / hit Chicken Licken
있어.   하늘의 한 조각이 /   치킨 리킨의 머리를 쳤어, /

on the head, / so we are going / to tell the King."
그래서 우리는 가는 중이야 /   왕에게 말하려고."

Ducky Lucky **flapped** her wings / in surprise / when
덕키 럭키는 날개를 퍼덕거렸어요 / 놀라서 /

she heard this news.
이 소식을 듣고.

"How **awful**," / she said in a **worried** voice.
"정말 끔찍해라," / 덕키 럭키는 걱정하는 목소리로 말했어요.

"May I come with you / to tell the King, / Chicken
"너희들과 함께 가도 되니 / 왕에게 말하려고, / 치킨 리킨?"

Licken?"

Words

• flap (날개를) 퍼덕거리다 • awful 끔찍한, 지독한

• worried 걱정하는, 걱정스러워 하는

"Of course you may," / said Chicken Licken, / and
"물론 그래도 좋지," /　　　　　　　치킨 리킨이 말했어요, /

so Ducky Lucky got out of the pond / and joined
그래서 덕키 럭키는 연못에서 나와 /　　　　　치킨 리킨과 코키 로키에

Chicken Licken and Cocky Locky / on their way /
합류했어요 /　　　　　　　　　　가는 중이었던 /

to see the King.
왕을 만나러.

Very soon, / the three travellers spied Goosey Lucy
곧, / 세 여행자들은 구시 루시를 봤어요 /

/ waddling towards them / on the path.
그들 쪽으로 어기적어기적 걸어오고 있는 / 길에서.

"Goosey Lucy," / called out Ducky Lucky / as soon
"구시 루시," / 덕키 럭키가 소리쳤어요 / 친구를 보자마

as she saw her friend, / "you must come quickly, /
자, / "넌 빨리 와야 해, /

the sky is falling down."
하늘이 무너지고 있어."

track 19

"Yes," / said Chicken Licken, / "a piece of it fell / on
"그렇고말고," / 치킨 리킨이 말했어요, / "하늘의 한 조각이 떨어졌어 /

my head. We are going / to tell the King."
내 머리에. 우리는 가는 중이야 / 왕에게 말하려고."

"Good Heavens!" / cried Goosey Lucy.
"저런!" / 구시 루시가 소리쳤어요.

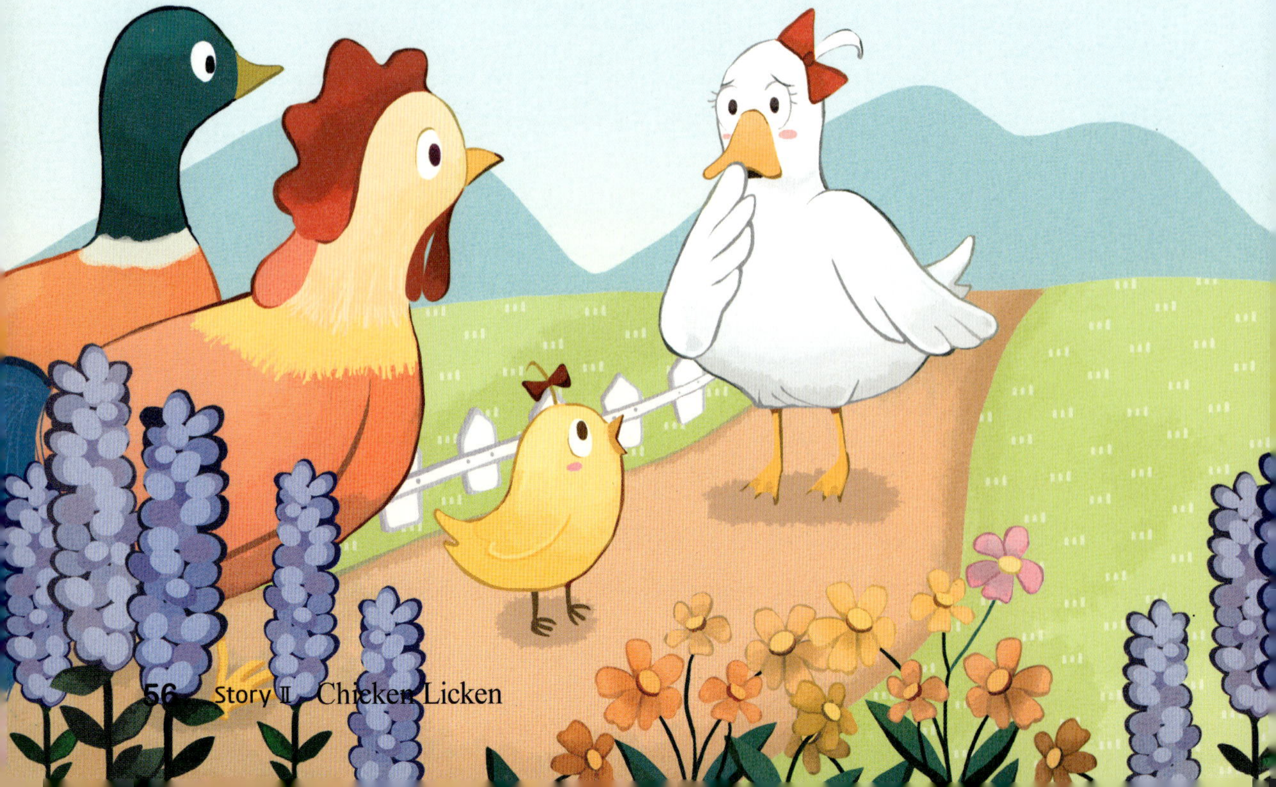

“I would like to come with you / to tell the King /
“나도 너희들과 함께 가고 싶어 /   왕에게 말하러 /

about that.”

그 일에 대해.”

“Of course, Goosey Lucy, / the more the merrier,” /
“좋고말고, 구시 루시야, /   더 많을수록 더 즐거우니까,” /

said Cocky Locky, / patting her on the back.
코키 로키가 말했어요, /   구시 루시의 등을 두드리면서.

1. 다음 단어 중 밑줄친 부분의 발음이 나머지 셋과 <u>다른</u> 것을 고르세요.

① Ⓐ d<u>u</u>st Ⓑ r<u>u</u>sh Ⓒ f<u>u</u>ll Ⓓ r<u>u</u>b

② Ⓐ ac<u>o</u>rn Ⓑ cl<u>o</u>nk Ⓒ p<u>o</u>nd Ⓓ g<u>o</u>bble

③ Ⓐ scr<u>a</u>tch Ⓑ spl<u>a</u>sh Ⓒ fl<u>a</u>p Ⓓ <u>a</u>wful

④ Ⓐ h<u>i</u>t Ⓑ f<u>i</u>ne Ⓒ l<u>i</u>p Ⓓ w<u>i</u>ng

2. 다음 문장이 주어진 의미가 될 수 있도록 보기에서 알맞은 단어를 골라 써 넣으세요.

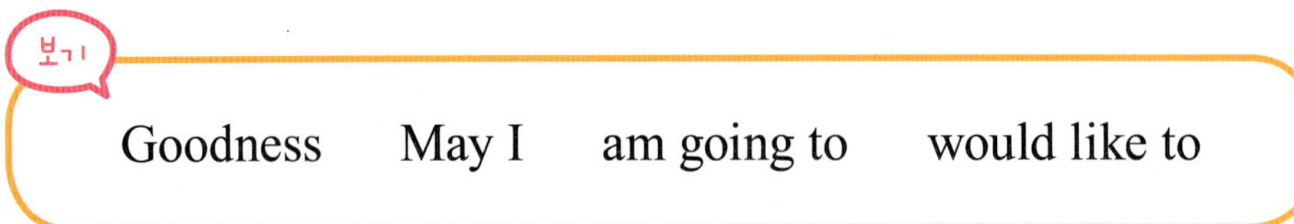

① 난 왕에게 말<u>하려고</u> <u>가는 중이야</u>.

➡ I ________________ tell the King.

② "어머나, 치킨 리킨, 심각하구나."

➡ "________________, Chicken Licken, that does sound serious."

③ "왕에게 말하려고 너희들과 함께 가도 <u>되니</u>, 치킨 리킨?"

➡ "________________ come with you to tell the King, Chicken Licken?"

④ "나도 너희들과 함께 왕에게 그 일에 대해 말하러 가고 <u>싶어</u>."

➡ "I ________________ come with you to tell the King about that."

3. 다음 녹음을 듣고, 보기에서 빈칸에 알맞은 단어를 골라 써 넣으세요.

> travellers   splashing   scratching   fine day

① Once upon a time, Chicken Licken was __________ around in the dust of the farmyard looking for something tasty to eat.

② "Where are you going on this __________?"

③ They had not got very far when they met Ducky Lucky, who was __________ around in the pond.

④ Very soon, the three __________ spied Goosey Lucy waddling towards them on the path.

1. ①-ⓒ / ②-Ⓐ / ③-Ⓓ / ④-Ⓑ
2. ① am going to ② Goodness ③ May I ④ would like to
3. ① scratching ② fine day ③ splashing ④ travellers

Chapter 2

Chicken Licken now / had quite a procession /
이제 치킨 리킨은 /   긴 행렬이 있었고 /

following her / on her way to see the King, / and
치킨 리킨을 따라가는 /   왕을 만나러 가고 있는, /

soon enough / there was one more.
곧 /   한 마리가 추가되었어요.

Turkey Lurkey was clucking and gobbling to
터키 러키는 꼬꼬댁거리며 고르륵고르륵 하는 소리를 내고 있었어요 /

himself / when he saw / his friends pass him, / all
                그가 보았을 때 /   친구들이 지나가는 것을, /

walking and waddling / very fast.
모두 걷거나 뒤뚱뒤뚱거리며 걸으면서 /   매우 빠르게.

"Hello there, everyone. Where are you all rushing

off to?"

"이봐, 여러분.　　　　　　어디로 너희들은 황급하게 가고 있니?"

Turkey Lurkey called after them.

터키 러키가 그들 뒤에서 불렀어요.

Chicken Licken, Cocky Locky, Ducky Lucky and
치킨 리킨, 코키 로키, 덕키 럭키와

Goosey Lucy turned their heads / and called back, /
구시 루시는 고개를 돌리며 /　　　　　　대답했어요, /

all at the same time, / "The sky is falling.
모두 동시에, /　　　　　　"하늘이 무너지고 있어.

We are going / to tell the King."
우리는 가는 중이야 /　　　왕에게 말하러."

Turkey Lurkey gasped / when he heard this.
터키 러키는 숨이 턱 막혔어요 /　　　이 소식을 듣자.

"This is terrible," / he said.
"끔찍한 일이야," /　　　그는 말했어요.

"Wait. Let me come with you," / and off he ran / to
"기다려, 너희들과 함께 갈게," /　　　　　　　　그리고 그는 빠르게 출발을 했어요 /

catch up with / the others.
따라잡으려고 /　　　　다른 무리를.

Words

- gasp 숨이 턱 막히다 • catch up with 따라잡다

After a while, / Chicken Licken, Cocky Locky,
잠시 후에, /   치킨 리킨, 코키 로키,

Ducky Lucky, Goosey Lucy and Turkey Lurkey /
덕키 럭키, 구시 루시와 터키 러키는 /

came to a big wood / full of tall trees.
큰 숲에 도착했어요 /   큰 나무로 빽빽한.

As they would soon find out, / it was in this wood /
그들이 곧 알게 되듯, /   바로 이 숲 속이었어요 /

that Foxy Loxy lived.
폭시 록시가 살고 있는.

Words
• after a while 잠시 후에 • full of ~로 가득찬 • find out ~을 알아내다

track 23

Foxy Loxy saw / the group of travellers coming /
폭시 록시는 봤고 / 여행자들의 무리가 다가오고 있는 것을 /

towards him / through the wood, / and he stepped
그에게 / 숲을 지나, / 그는 나왔어요 /

out / from behind a tree / into their path.
나무 뒤에서 / 길로.

"Well well, what have we here?" / he said, / in his
"이런 이런, 여기 있는 것들이 뭐야?" / 그가 말했어요, /

smooth, syrupy voice.
부드럽고, 달콤한 목소리로.

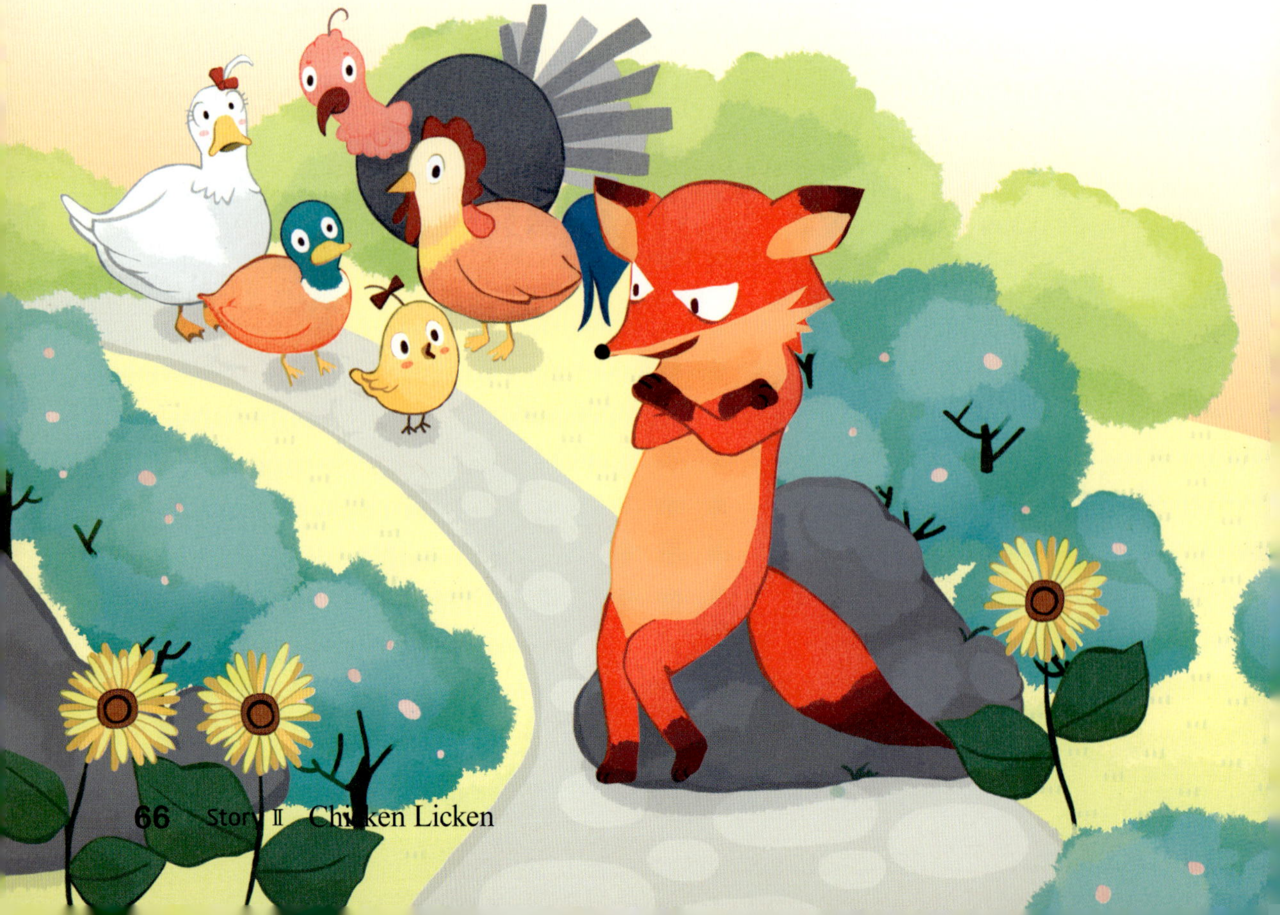

"Oh!" / said Chicken Licken, / who was a bit
"오!" /   치킨 리킨이 말했어요, /   약간 놀랐지만.

startled.

"Hello there Foxy Loxy. The most terrible thing has
"저기 안녕 폭시 록시.   가장 끔찍한 일이 일어났어.

happened. A piece of the sky fell / on my head, /
        하늘의 한 조각이 떨어졌거든 /   내 머리에, /

and we are going / to tell the King / about it."
그래서 우리는 가고 있는 중이야 / 왕에게 말하려고 /   그 일에 대해."

A smile spread / over Foxy Loxy's sly face / when
미소가 번졌어요 /   폭시 록시의 교활한 얼굴에 /   이 말을 듣자.

he heard this.

"Yes, / you must tell the King, / straight away," /
"그렇고말고, / 왕에게 말해야지, /   지체 없이," /

he said.
그는 말했어요.

"Come with me. I know a shortcut / that will get
"나와 함께 가자.   내가 지름길을 알고 있어 /   너희들을 궁전에 도착하게

you to the palace / much faster."
할 /   휠씬 더 빨리."

Chicken Licken, Cocky Locky, Ducky Lucky,
치킨 리킨, 코키 로키, 덕키 럭키,

Goosey Lucy and Turkey Lurkey were very grateful
구시 루시와 터키 러키는 매우 감사했어요 /

/ for Foxy Loxy's help.
폭시 록시의 도움에.

They followed him / through the trees, / as he led
그들은 그를 따라갔어요 /　　　나무들 사이로, /　　　여우가 그들을 데리고

them / deeper and deeper into the wood.
갈 때 /　　숲 속으로 더욱 더 깊숙이.

Soon, / they came to the entrance / to a cave.
곧, /　　　그들은 입구에 도착했어요 /　　　동굴로 향하는.

Words

- spread 번지다, 퍼지다 • sly 교활한 • straight away 지체 없이, 즉시

- shortcut 지름길 • grateful 감사하는, 고마워하는 • lead 데리고 가다

- entrance 입구 • cave 동굴

"If you go through this tunnel / you will come out /
"너희들이 이 굴을 통과하면 /　　　　나올 거야 /

right next to the palace, / and you will be able to tell
바로 궁전 옆으로, /　　　　그러면 왕에게 말할 수 있을 거야 /

the King / about the sky falling down," / said Foxy
　　　　하늘이 무너진 사건에 대해," /　　　　폭시 록시가 말했어

Loxy.
요.

Chicken Licken, Cocky Locky, Ducky Lucky,
치킨 리킨, 코키 로키, 덕키 럭키,

Goosey Lucy and Turkey Lurkey thanked him, /
구시 루시와 터키 러키는 감사를 표하고, /

and went inside.
안으로 들어갔어요.

Foxy Loxy licked his lips / with his pink tongue, /

폭시 록시는 입술을 핥고 /　　　　　그의 분홍색 혀로, /

and followed them / into the cave.

그들을 따라갔어요 /　　　　　동굴 안으로.

By the time Chicken Licken and her friends realized
치킨 리킨과 그의 친구들이 깨달았을 때 /

/ that they had been tricked, / it was too late.
속았다고, /   너무 늦었어요.

The King was never told / that the sky was falling
왕은 결코 듣지 못했고 /   하늘이 무너지고 있다는 소식을, /

down, / and the only one to come out of the cave /
그리고 동굴에서 나온 유일한 자는 /

a few days later / was a very full and very fat Foxy
며칠 후에 /   매우 배부르고 살진 폭시 록시였어요.

Loxy.

Key Expression
'be told'는 '듣다'라고 해석한답니다.

The King was never told / that the sky was falling down.
왕은 듣지 못했어요 /   하늘이 무너지고 있다는 소식을.

Words
• realize 깨닫다 • trick 속이다

Mini Test 2

1. 비슷한 의미를 가진 단어를 찾아 연결해 보세요.

① startled　　　　　　　　　　　　Ⓐ ran off

② go off　　　　　　　　　　　　　Ⓑ land

③ straight away　　　　　　　　　Ⓒ at once

④ fall　　　　　　　　　　　　　　Ⓓ surprise

2. 다음 문장이 주어진 의미가 될 수 있도록 보기에서 알맞은 단어를 골라 써 넣으세요.

> 보기
>
> Let me　　rushing off to　　was never told　　be able to

① 너희들 모두 어디로 황급하게 가고 있니?

➡ Where are you all ________________ ?

② 너희들과 함께 갈래.

➡ ________________ come with you.

③ 왕에게 하늘이 무너진 사건에 대해 말할 수 있을 거야.

➡ You will ________________ tell the King about the sky falling down.

74

④ 왕은 하늘이 무너지고 있다는 소식을 결코 <u>듣지 못했어요</u>.

➡ The King _________________________ that the sky was falling down.

3. 다음 녹음을 듣고, 보기에서 빈칸에 알맞은 단어를 골라 써 넣으세요.

> shortcut   find out   startled   gobbling

① Turkey Lurkey was clucking and _____________ to himself when he saw his friends pass him, all walking and waddling very fast.

② As they would soon _____________, it was in this wood that Foxy Loxy lived.

③ "Oh!" said Chicken Licken, who was a bit _____________.

④ "Come with me. I know a _____________ that will get you to the palace much faster."

1. ①-ⓓ / ②-ⓐ / ③-ⓒ / ④-ⓑ
2. ① rushing off to ② Let me ③ be able to ④ was never told
3. ① gobbling ② find out ③ startled ④ shortcut

Chicken Licken

Once upon a time, Chicken Licken was scratching
around in the dust of the farmyard looking for
something tasty to eat.
Suddenly, an acorn fell from a nearby tree and landed
on her head with a clonk.

"Oh my!" squawked Chicken Licken,
rubbing her head. "The sky is falling down.
I must go and tell the King at once."
So off she went, as fast as her short little legs would
carry her.

Before very long, she met Cocky Locky.
"Hello there, Chicken Licken," said Cocky Locky.
"Where are you going on this fine day?"

"It is not a fine day at all, Cocky Locky. The sky is
falling down. A piece of it hit me on my head, and I
am going to tell the King."
"Goodness, Chicken Licken, that does sound serious,"
said Cocky Locky, frowning.

"May I come with you?"

"Of course you may," said Chicken
Licken to Cocky Locky, and off
they went to see the King and tell
him that the sky was falling.

They had not got very far when they met Ducky
Lucky, who was splashing around in the pond.

"Hello there, you two," said Ducky Lucky to Chicken
Licken and Cocky Locky.
"Where are you going in such a hurry?"

"Oh, Ducky Lucky," said Cocky Locky, "the sky is
falling down. A piece of it hit Chicken Licken on the
head, so we are going to tell the King."

Ducky Lucky flapped her wings in surprise when she
heard this news.
"How awful," she said in a worried voice.
"May I come with you to tell the King, Chicken
Licken?"

"Of course you may," said Chicken Licken, and so Ducky Lucky got out of the pond and joined Chicken Licken and Cocky Locky on their way to see the King. Very soon, the three travellers spied Goosey Lucy waddling towards them on the path.

"Goosey Lucy," called out Ducky Lucky as soon as she saw her friend, "you must come quickly, the sky is falling down."

"Yes," said Chicken Licken, "a piece of it fell on my head. We are going to tell the King."

"Good Heavens!" cried Goosey Lucy.
"I would like to come with you to tell the King about that."

"Of course, Goosey Lucy, the more the merrier," said Cocky Locky, patting her on the back.

Chicken Licken now had quite a procession following her on her way to see the King, and soon enough there was one more. Turkey Lurkey was clucking and gobbling to himself when he saw his friends pass him, all walking and waddling very fast.

"Hello there, everyone. Where are you all rushing off to?"
Turkey Lurkey called after them. Chicken Licken, Cocky Locky, Ducky Lucky and Goosey Lucy turned their heads and called back, all at the same time, "The sky is falling. We are going to tell the King."

Turkey Lurkey gasped when he heard this.
"This is terrible," he said.
"Wait. Let me come with you," and off he ran to catch up with the others.

After a while, Chicken Licken, Cocky Locky, Ducky
Lucky, Goosey Lucy and Turkey Lurkey came to a big
wood full of tall trees.
As they would soon find out, it was in this wood that
Foxy Loxy lived.

Foxy Loxy saw the group of travellers coming towards
him through the wood, and he stepped out from behind
a tree into their path.
"Well well, what have we here?" he said, in his
smooth, syrupy voice.

"Oh!" said Chicken Licken, who was a bit startled.
"Hello there Foxy Loxy. The most terrible thing has
happened. A piece of the sky fell on my head, and we
are going to tell the King about it."

A smile spread over Foxy Loxy's sly face when he
heard this.
"Yes, you must tell the King, straight away," he said.
"Come with me. I know a shortcut that will get you to
the palace much faster."

Chicken Licken, Cocky Locky, Ducky Lucky, Goosey
Lucy and Turkey Lurkey were very grateful for Foxy
Loxy's help.
They followed him through the trees, as he led them
deeper and deeper into the wood.

Soon, they came to the entrance to a cave.
"If you go through this tunnel you will come out right
next to the palace, and you will be able to tell the King
about the sky falling down," said Foxy Loxy.
Chicken Licken, Cocky Locky, Ducky Lucky, Goosey
Lucy and Turkey Lurkey thanked him, and went
inside.

Foxy Loxy licked his lips with his pink tongue, and
followed them into the cave.

By the time Chicken Licken and her friends realized
that they had been tricked, it was too late.
The King was never told that the sky was falling
down, and the only one to come out of the cave a few
days later was a very full and very fat Foxy Loxy.

Final Test

1. 다음 빈칸에 들어갈 알맞은 단어를 골라 ◯표 하세요.

① A piece of it hit Chicken Licken (on / to) the head.

② "Of course, Goosey Lucy, the more the (merry / merrier)," said Cocky Locky, patting her on the back.

③ They followed him through the trees, as he led them deeper (or / and) deeper into the wood.

2. 다음 문장을 직독직해 해 보세요.

① Ducky Lucky got out of the pond / and joined Chicken Licken and Cocky Locky /

➡

on their way to see the King.

➡

② By the time Chicken Licken and her friends realized /

➡

that they had been tricked, / it was too late.

➡

③ The only one to come out of the cave / a few days later / was a very full and very fat Foxy Loxy.

3. 다음 문장을 영작해 보세요.

① 넌 빨리 와야 해, / 하늘이 무너지고 있어.

➥

② 폭시 록시는 봤어요 / 여행자들의 무리가 다가오고 있는 것을 /

➥

그에게 / 숲을 지나.

➥

③ 미소가 번졌어요 / 폭시 록시의 교활한 얼굴에 / 이 말을 듣자.

➥

Answer
1. ① on ② merrier ③ and
2. ① 덕키 럭키는 연못에서 나와 / 치킨 리킨과 코키 로키에 합류했어요 / 가는 중이었던 / 왕을 만나러.
② 치킨 리킨과 그의 친구들이 깨달았을 때 / 속았다고, / 너무 늦었어요.
③ 동굴에서 나온 유일한 자는 / 며칠 후에 / 매우 배부르고 살진 폭시 록시였어요.
3. ① You must come quickly, / the sky is falling down.
② Foxy Loxy saw / the group of travellers coming / towards him / through the wood.
③ A smile spread / over Foxy Loxy's sly face / when he heard this.

4. 다음 문장이 주어진 의미가 될 수 있도록 빈칸에 알맞은 말을 써 넣어 보세요.

① "그렇게 서둘러 어디로 가고 있니?"

➡ "Where are you going ___________________?"

② 덕키 럭키는 치킨 리킨과 코키 로키가 왕을 만나러 가는 길에 합류했어요.

➡ Duchy Lucky joined Chicken Licken and Cocky Locky ___________________ to see the King.

③ "구시 루시," 덕키 럭키는 그녀의 친구를 보자마자 소리쳤어요.

➡ "Goosey Lucy," called out Ducky Lucky ___________________ she saw her friend.

5. 다음 문장이 본문의 내용과 맞으면 T, 틀리면 F에 ✔표 하세요.

① A piece of sky hit Chicken Licken on her head.

(T / F)

② Chicken Licken and her friends went off to tell the king that the sky was falling.

(T / F)

③ Foxy Loxy wanted to join Chicken Licken's, but they didn't agree.

(T / F)

6. 다음 빈칸에 들어갈 알맞은 말을 보기에서 골라 이야기를 완성해 보세요.

보기

| tricked | full of | nearby | cave | at once |
| led | realized | entrance | landed | acorn |

Once upon a time, an ①___________ fell from ②___________
tree and ③___________ on Chicken Licken's head.
She thought it was a piece of the sky and the sky was falling,
so off she went to tell the king ④___________ .

On her way to see king, she met her friends, Cocky Locky,
Ducky Lucky, Goosey Lucy and Turkey Lurkey.

When they came to a big wood ⑤___________ tall trees,
where Foxy Loxy lived. Foxy Loxy ⑥___________ them into the
wood and came to the ⑦___________ to a ⑧___________ .
Foxy Loxy was so happy because all of them would be his food.

Finally, Chicken Licken and her friends ⑨___________ that
they had been ⑩___________ , but it was too late.
The king was never told that the sky was falling down,
and we couldn't see them any more.

Answer
4. ① in such a hurry ② on their way ③ as soon as
5. ① F ② T ③ F
6. ① acorn ② nearby ③ landed ④ at once
　⑤ entrance ⑥ cave ⑦ full of ⑧ led ⑨ realized ⑩ tricked

Index

a stream of 한 줄로 늘어선

acorn 도토리

activity 활동

after a while 잠시 후에

aid (특정 인물에 대한) 도움

angrily 노하여, 성나서

at once 당장

at the top of one's voice
목청껏, 최대의 목소리로

awful 끔찍한, 지독한

before too long 머지않아, 곧

below 아래에

bored 따분한, 지루한

burst out laughing 웃음을 터뜨리다

call after 뒤에서 부르다

catch up with 따라잡다

cave 동굴

clonk 쿵하는 소리

cluck 꼬꼬댁거리다

complain 불평하다

countryside 시골, 지방

decide to ~하기로 결심하다

drive ~ away
~을 쫓아내다, 몰아내다

dust 흙먼지

entertain 즐겁게 하다

entrance 입구

extra 추가의

farmyard 농가의 안마당

feast 마음껏 먹다

find out ~을 알아내다

flap (날개를) 퍼덕거리다

flock (양의) 떼, 무리

frown 얼굴을 찌푸리다

full of ~로 가득찬

gasp 숨이 턱 막히다

get one's breath back 숨을 돌리다

get out (of) (~에서) 떠나다

gobble 고르륵고르륵 하는 소리를 내다

gobble up 잡아먹다

good heavens 이런, 큰일이군, 맙소사

goodness
(놀람을 나타내며) 와, 어머나

grateful 감사하는, 고마워하는

graze 풀을 뜯어먹다

have had enough of
진절머리가 나다, 싫증이 나다

hillside 산의 중턱

hit 치다, 때리다

hurry 서두름, 급함

hurt 아프다

join 합류하다

land 떨어지다, 착륙하다

lead 데리고 가다

lick one's lips 입술을 핥다

look 표정

look after 돌보다

look for 찾다

manage to 겨우(간신히) ~하다

meal 식사

merry 즐거운

naughty 장난꾸러기의

nearby 근처의

once again 또 다시, 한 번 더

onto 위에

pant 헐떡거리다

pat 쓰다듬다

path 길

play a trick on ~에게 장난을 하다

pond 연못

procession 행렬

puff (숨을) 헐떡이다

quickly 빨리

race (심장이) 뛰다

reach ~에 이르다

realize 깨닫다, 알아차리다

reluctantly 마지못해, 어쩔 수 없이

resist 참다

rub 문지르다

rush off to 급히 ~에 가다

scratch around 이리저리 헤집다

serious 심각한

shake head 고개를 젓다

shortcut 지름길

shout 외치다

shut (문이) 닫히다

slink 살금살금 가다

sly 교활한

smooth (소리가) 부드러운

splash (물에서) 첨벙거리다, 물을 튀기다

spot 장소, 지점

spread 번지다, 퍼지다

spy 보다

squawk 꽥꽥거리다

startled 깜짝 놀란

step out 나가다

straight away 지체 없이, 즉시

sure enough 예상한 대로, 예측한대로

syrupy 달콤한

tasty 맛있다

tempting 솔깃한, 구미가 당기는

thank 감사를 표하다

tire of 싫증을 내다

towards ~쪽으로

traveller 여행자

trick 속이다

tunnel (동물이 사는) 굴

useful 도움이 되는

village (시골) 마을

villager 마을 사람

waddle 어기적어기적 걷다

watch over 지키다

worried 걱정하는, 걱정스러워 하는